All Through My Town

Jean Reidy   illustrated by Leo Timmers

BLOOMSBURY

LONDON   NEW DELHI   NEW YORK   SYDNEY

Bloomsbury Publishing, London, New Delhi, New York and Sydney
First published in Great Britain in 2013 by Bloomsbury Publishing Plc
50 Bedford Square, London, WC1B 3DP

First published in the US in 2013 by Bloomsbury Books for Young Readers
175 Fifth Avenue, New York, New York 10010

A CIP catalogue record of this book is available from the British Library
conform to the environmental regulations of the country of origin.

ISBN 978 1 4088 3860 0

Printed in China
1 3 5 7 9 10 8 6 4 2

All papers used by Bloomsbury Publishing are natural, recyclable products made from
wood grown in well-managed forests. The manufacturing processes conform to the environmental regulations of the country of origin

www.bloomsbury.com

To Mike, my wingman on all my adventures,
whether they be halfway around the world
or just around the town —J. R.

For Gina, without whom I would be lost —L. T.

Rising, waking.

Bread is baking.

School bus honks its horn.

Seeding, sowing.
Cockerel crowing.

Counting cobs of corn.

Pancakes flipping.
Cutting, clipping.

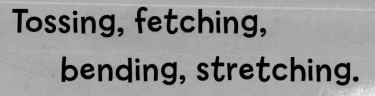

Tossing, fetching,
bending, stretching.

Brushing, shaving.
Goodbye waving . . .

my town in the morn.

Shopping, sacking,
sorting, stacking . . .

rows so nice and neat.

School bells ringing.
Reading, singing,

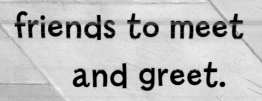

friends to meet
and greet.

Spraying, sweeping, backing, beeping.

Starting, stopping,
tram car hopping.

Blazing, dashing.
Red lights flashing!
My town's busy street.

Stamping,
mailing,
painting,
nailing,

ladder up and down.

Whistling, wheeling,
helping, healing.
Laugh away a frown.

Shelving, shushing.
Fountain gushing.

Swinging, lunching.
Cookie munching.

Peeking, peeping,
someone's sleeping . . .

All through my town.

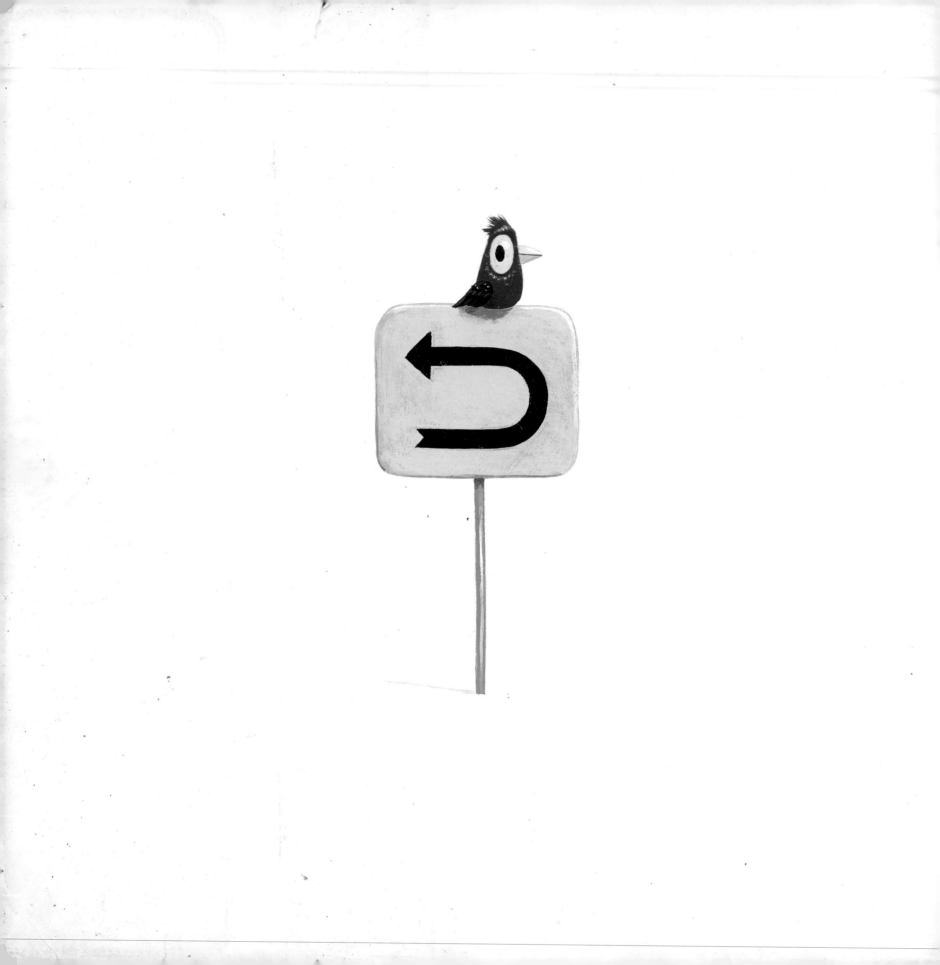